LITTLE SIMON

Simon & Schuster Building, Rockefeller Center

1230 Avenue of the Americas, New York, New York 10020

Manufactured in Singapore   10 9 8 7 6 5 4 3 2

Library of Congress Cataloging-in-Publication Data

Turtles / the Cousteau Society.   p.   cm.   Summary: Describes the physical characteristics, behavior, and life cycle of the green turtle.   1. Green turtle—Juvenile literature.   [1. Green turtle.   2. Turtles.]   I. Cousteau Society.   QL666.C536T87 1992
597.92—dc20   91-32184   CIP

ISBN: 0-671-77059-4

The Cousteau Society

TURTLES

LITTLE SIMON

Published by Simon & Schuster

New York London Toronto Sydney Tokyo Singapore

THE GREEN SEA TURTLE

Reptile

Weight and size
Hatchling: 8 ounces, $1\frac{1}{2}$ inches
Adult: 440 pounds, 4 feet

Lifespan
Up to 100-150 years

Food
Plants and small animals

Reproduction
Mates under water every 3-4 years.
Lays 100 eggs in the sand.
Eggs hatch after 8 weeks.

Wide migratory ranges.

Populations threatened by fishing, pollution,
poaching, habitat loss.

These are sea turtles,
swimming protected by their thick, hard shells.

The turtle has large, flat flippers that help it
swim gracefully.

Turtles leave the sea to dig their nests on the beach.

The nest is ready. The turtle lays her round white eggs.

Morning comes. The eggs are safely buried, and

the turtle slowly returns to the sea.

It's time! Baby turtles hatch

and rush to the water.

Helpless, the tiny turtle hides until it is big

enough to explore the sea.